KT-503-746

The
WIT & WISDOM
— of —
TYRION
LANNISTER

HarperCollins*Publishers*
77–85 Fulham Palace Road,
Hammersmith, London W6 8JB

www.harpercollins.co.uk

Published by Harper*Voyager*
An imprint of HarperCollins*Publishers* 2013
I

A catalogue record for this book
is available from the British Library

ISBN: 978-0-00-753232-2

Printed and bound in China

The WIT & WISDOM of TYRION LANNISTER

By George R.R. Martin

Illustrated *by* Jonty Clark

HARPER
Voyager

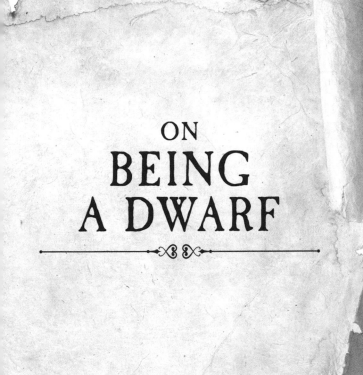

ON
BEING
A DWARF

All dwarfs are bastards in
their father's eyes.

What joy to be a dwarf.

I was born. I lived. I am guilty of being a dwarf, I confess it. And no matter how many times my good father forgave me, I have persisted in my infamy.

I have been called many things but
giant is seldom one of them.

9

No one fears a dwarf.

All dwarfs may be bastards, yet not
all bastards need be dwarfs.

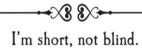

I'm short, not blind.

16

Do you think I might stand taller
in black?

17

I am malformed, scarred, and small,
but . . . abed, when the candles are blown
out, I am made no worse than other men.
In the dark, I am the Knight of Flowers.

Dwarfs are a jape of the gods,
but men make eunuchs.

They say I'm half a man. What does
that make the lot of you?

I have a tender spot in my heart for cripples and bastards and broken things.

The gods must have been drunk
when they got to me.

I only need half my wits to be a
match for you.

I had dreamt enough for one small life.
And of such follies: love, justice, friendship, glory.
As well dream of being tall.

It may be good luck to rub the head of
a dwarf, but it is even better luck to suck
on a dwarf's cock.

ON
THE POWER
OF WORDS

My mind is my weapon. My brother
has his sword, King Robert has his warhammer,
and I have my mind . . . and a mind needs books as
a sword needs a whetstone if it is to keep its edge.

Duck has his sword, I my quill
and parchment.

Sleep is good. And books are better.

Let them see that their words can cut
you and you'll never be free of the mockery.
If they want to give you a name, take it
and make it your own. Then they can't
hurt you with it any more.

Guard your tongue before it
digs your grave.

Words are wind.

When you tear out a man's tongue, you are not proving him a liar, you are only telling the world that you fear what he might say.

ON
ROMANCE

I would prefer a whore who is reasonably young, with as pretty a face as you can find. If she has washed sometime this year, I shall be glad. If she hasn't, wash her.

Shy maids are my favourite sort. Aside from wanton ones . . . but sometimes the ugliest ones are the hungriest once abed.

My own father could not love me.
Why would you if not for gold?

A man grows weary of having no
lovers but his fingers.

I plant my little seeds just as
often as I can.

Your Grace, if you take my tongue,
you will leave me no way at all to pleasure
this sweet wife you gave me.

Sleep with Lollys? I'd sooner cut it off
and feed it to the goats.

With whores, the young ones smell much better,
but the old ones know more tricks.

A dwarf's cock has magical powers.

ON
FAMILY
VALUES

A Lannister always pays his debts.

I never bet against my family.

Kindness is not a habit with us Lannisters, I fear,
but I know I have some somewhere.

Hard hands and no sense of humour
makes for a bad marriage.

I should say something, but what?
Pardon me, Father, but it's our brother
she wants to marry.

Kinslaying is dry work. It gives a man a thirst.

My sister has mistaken me for
a mushroom. She keeps me in the
dark and feeds me shit.

The man who kills his own
blood is cursed forever in the
sight of gods and men.

I learned long ago that it is considered
rude to vomit on your brother.

Kinslaying was not enough, I needed a cunt
and wine to seal my ruin.

I have never liked you, Cersei, but you were
my own sister, so I never did you harm.
You've ended that. I will hurt you for this.
I don't know how yet, but give me time. A day
will come when you think you are safe and happy,
and suddenly your joy will turn to ashes in your
mouth, and you will know the debt is paid.

ON
THE HUMAN
CONDITION

❧

The gods are blind. And men see
only what they wish.

Life is a japc. Yours, mine, everyone's.

Why is it that when one man builds a wall,
the next man immediately needs to know what's
on the other side?

Death is so terribly final, while life is
full of possibilities.

An honest kiss, a little kindness, everyone deserves that much, however big or small.

Every fool loves to hear that
he's important.

Never forget who you are, for surely
the world will not. Make it your strength.
Then it can never be your weakness.
Armour yourself in it, and it will
never be used to hurt you.

A little honest loathing might be refreshing,
like a tart wine after too much sweet.

We all need to be mocked from
time to time, lest we start to take
ourselves too seriously.

If there is food I eat it, in case there
is none on the morrow

Age makes ruins of us all.

There has never been a slave who
did not choose to be a slave. Their choice
may be between bondage and death,
but the choice is always there.

We are all going to die.

ON
MUSIC

Never believe anything you hear in a song.

If I am ever Hand again the first thing
I'll do is hang all the singers.

I have killed mothers, fathers,
nephews, lovers, men and women, kings
and whores. A singer once annoyed me,
so I had the bastard stewed.

ON
FOOD AND
DRINK

I've heard the food in hell is wretched.

Being randy is the next best thing
to being drunk.

I am not fond of eating horse.
Particularly my horse.

Someone should tell the cooks that turnip isn't a meat.

If you drink enough fire wine perhaps
you'll dream of dragons.

ON
KINGSHIP

All sorts of people are calling themselves kings these days.

Crowns do queer things to the
heads beneath them.

My nephew is not fit to sit a privy,
let alone the Iron Throne.

Power is a mummer's trick.

Kings are falling like leaves
this autumn.

ON
REALPOLITIK

———❦———

Some allies are more dangerous
than enemies.

You can buy a man with gold, but only
blood and steel will keep him true.

Schemes are like fruit, they require
a certain ripening.

It all goes back and back, to our mothers and fathers and theirs before them. We are puppets dancing on the strings of those who came before us, and one day our own children will take up our strings and dance in our steads.

Rebellion makes for queer bedfellows.

When winter comes, the realm will starve.

THE ART
OF WAR

Gold has its uses, but wars are
won with iron.

I sit a chair better than a horse, and I'd
sooner hold a wine goblet than a battleaxe.
All that about the thunder of the drums, sunlight
flashing on armour, magnificent destriers snorting
and prancing? Well, the drums gave me headaches,
the sunlight flashing on my armour cooked me up
like a harvest day goose, and those magnificent
destriers shit everywhere.

How many Dornishmen does it take to start a war? Only one.

He's as useful as nipples on a breastplate.

Men fight more fiercely for a king
who shares their peril than one who
hides behind his mother's skirts.

If a man paints a target on his chest, he should expect that sooner or later someone will loose an arrow at him.

A sword through the bowels.
A sure cure for constipation.

Knights know only one way to solve a
problem. They couch their lance and charge.
A dwarf has a different way of looking
at the world.

This is the way of war. The small folk
are slaughtered, while highborn are held
to ransom. Remind me to thank the
gods that I was born a Lannister.

THE ART OF SAVING YOUR SKIN

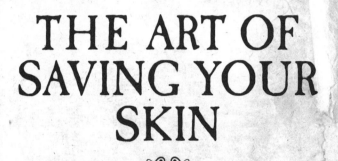

Courage and folly are cousins,
or so I've heard.

I'm terrified of my enemies,
so I kill them all.

I decline to deliver any message that
might get me killed.

All this mistrust will sour your
stomach and keep you awake by night,
'tis true, but better that than the
long sleep that does not end.

Riding hard and fast by night is
a sure way to tumble down a mountain
and crack your skull.

THE ART OF LYING

Give me sweet lies, and keep your
bitter truths.

How did I lose my nose? I shoved it up
your wife's cunt and she bit it off.

The best lies are seasoned with
a bit of truth.

My mother loved me best of all her children, because I was so small. She nursed me at her breast till I was seven. That made my brothers jealous, so they stuffed me in a sack and sold me to a mummers' troupe. When I tried to run off, the master mummer cut off half my nose, so I had no choice but to go with them and learn to be amusing.

—◆❧ ❧◆—

The sow I ride is actually my sister. We have the
same nose, could you tell? A wizard cast
a spell on her, but if you give her a big wet kiss
she'll turn into a beautiful woman. The pity
is, once you get to know her, you'll want to
kiss her again to turn her back.

Every touch a lie. I have paid her so much false coin that she half thinks she's rich.

You'd be astonished at what a boy can
make of a few lies, fifty pieces of silver,
and a drunken septon.

Half-truths are worth more than
outright lies.

ON
DRAGONS,
AND OTHER
MYTHS

※❦❦❦※

Next you will be offering me a suit of
magic armour and a palace in Valyria.

Even a stunted, twisted, ugly little boy
can look down over the world when he's
seated on a dragon's back.

Once a man has seen a dragon in flight,
let him stay home and tend his garden
in content, for this wide world has
no greater wonder.

It is never wise to tempt the dragons.

The Shrouded Lord is just a legend, no more real
than the ghost of Lann the Clever that some claim
haunts Casterley Rock.

Monsters are dangerous beasts.

ON
RELIGION

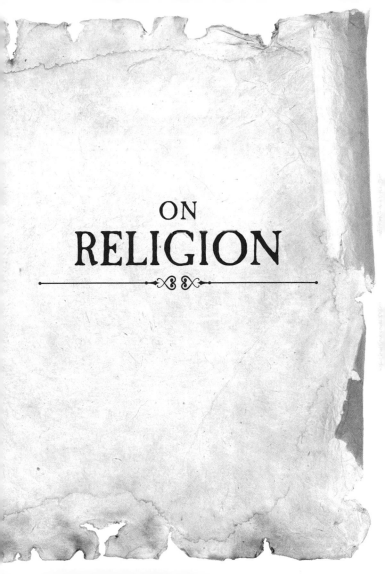

What sort of gods make rats and
plagues and dwarfs?

152

When I was a boy, my wet nurse told me
that one day, if men were good, the gods
would give the world a summer
without ending.

Light our fire and protect us from the dark, blah blah, light our way and keep us toasty warm, the night is dark and full of terrors, save us from the scary things, and blah blah blah some more . . .

Somewhere some god is laughing.

If there are gods to listen, they are
monstrous gods, who torment us for their sport.
Who else would make a world like this, so full of
bondage, blood, and pain?

The gods give with one hand and
take with the other.

If I could pray with my cock,
I would be much more religious.

Gods and wonders always appear,
to attend the birth of kings.